MW01172823

FIFI'S EROTIC BOUTIQUE
A Store of Pleasure

FIFI'S EROTIC

BOUTIQUE

A Store of Pleasure

by

ESMERALDA LINTNER

INTRODUCTION

Bonjour, Mesdames et Messieurs!
Guten Tag, meine Damen und Herren!
Good day, Ladies and Gentlemen!

I am Fifi Poofay! Welcome to my store of erotic fulfillment. You will find all that titillates and stimulates the sensual side of yourself. You have now entered into a world of all which is naughty and forbidden.

Each climax you have will bring you hours of pleasure and make you want more. Each groan and moan will excite even of those who are experts in foreplay, cunnilingus, fellatio,... you know, blow jobs! Consider this to be your home away from home. Spend one day with me and I'll make you hornier than hell. You will experience the world of lay, screw, shag, bang, bonk, hump, copulate, and last but not least, FORNICATE!

Come! The doors are open and welcome to all! Let me take you through my wacky and perverted tour of orgasms. As you enter into the main room here, to the left we have THE COCK IN THE CLOCK. Each hour when the clock strikes, this stiff bulging mushroom head protrudes outwards and squirts its heavenly *créme de la cum*!

Ooh-la-la! You're just in time: here it is, sticking out now. No jerking it off is necessary!

Next up we have our sexual delights which are all

1

mounted on our ass-cheek trays. They include DANNY'S DILDOS. They come in five fine fucking flavors: blow-berry, boner-nanner, choco-nuts-on-your-balls, virgin's-vanilla and screwing-strawberry. They not only fuck well but are tasty, too!

Over here to my right are Tina's Titillating Titties. They come in A to D sizes. Each titty comes with nipples. When you massage or rub them they become very hard and sensitive. It gives you the erotic sensation of those stiffening nipples you've heard about.

As we go to the back here, we have our inflatable animals. These we call the Butthole Bunnies. One can role play being either the top [giving] or bottom [receiving it in the ass], or what in French we call *le trou du cul* --- the butthole.

For more of an erotic sensation, may we recommend Lucy's Lube? It will assist you in lubricating the rabbit's furry hole and give you hours of butt-fucking fun.

Of course let's not forget our vaginas! We have our special flavor of the week: cucumber cunts.

There are other hot goodies that you can turn on with, but time does not allow me to elaborate. I have had many interesting clients come here seeking to fulfill their different sexual needs and desires. Let me share just a few examples with you.

1

Bob and Carol are a couple who lived out of town far away in the hills. They both came from very conservative families. They also were both sheltered, especially when it came to sexual matters --- those were strictly taboo.

I will never forget the story they shared with me. One day they both came in and wanted to buy a few sex items which would help them shed their inhibitions. They were so shy, and I could tell they didn't have much experience in sex. Bob asked, "What is that long rubber thing there --- the one with the double heads on it?"

I tried to keep from laughing, just smiling all the while. "That is what we call a dildo."

"Oh, I see," he responded enthusiastically. "I'll take that one. I'll also add those little rubber things there."

"Do you like plain or do you prefer flavors?" I asked.

"Flavors? Oh, wow! I'll take chocolate, please," he said politely.

He paid for the items and rushed home with Carol to try them out. Poor Bob, he had a package of rubbers and didn't know what to do with them. He sat there trying them on. He tried them on his finger, his mouth and nose. Then he blew one up like a balloon. Carol sat there and just laughed.

"Hon, what in heaven's name are you doin'?"

"Well," Bob replied, very frustrated, "I couldn't fit this rubber on my hand, so I thought I'd blow it up."

"What in the world for?"

"I thought I'd give it a blow job."

They next tried their dildo. Both of them were confused as hell. They didn't know which end went where. They faced each other, grabbed one end and stuck it in their mouths. Of course nothing happened. Carol said she had an idea. "Let's try sticking in each other asses."

Bob loved the idea. "Hold on," he exclaimed and reached over to grab the package of rubbers. He then started slipping one around the dildo.

"What in tarnation are you doin' with that there rubber?" Carol asked incredulously.

"I always heard," Bob replied with a straight face, "that one should always practice safe sex. I'm afraid one of us might get pregnant."

2

There is another interesting client I have catered to. All of us have our own kink, our own obsessions. This was a man of the cloth --- a priest, of all things!

Father Jake definitely had his own fetish. I affectionately called him The Jack-off Priest. The only way he could jerk off was in public, and it was in the confessional, of all places! This is what he loved to do and it was his way of getting off, you might say.

One day Father Jake came in, began looking the place over but was a little nervous. He didn't want it known that he came here for my, shall we say, *expert* advice. "Good day to you, Ma'am. I have a problem. I want to make this just between the two of us."

Leaning forward and cupping his hand at the side of his mouth while nervously glancing around, he whispered, "I just love to jerk off, especially when I'm listening to confessions. There's just something about hearing those naughty sins of the flesh. It's those sex stories that do it to me every time! I can't seem to keep my cock in my pants. I just whip out the ol' wiener and whack off." Catching his breath and trying not to sob, he added, "Lately, though, it seems that I just can't get it up."

Poor Father Jake! He couldn't get the ol' thing to stand up. I had an idea and went over to the section where I stored Lucy's Lube. I came back and handed it to him.

5

"God bless you, my child," he exclaimed gratefully. He paid me and hastily went to the church since it was Saturday afternoon and almost time for confessions to begin. This time he was prepared and properly equipped to hear those naughty activities and enjoy them to the fullest.

One young man came in and started confessing that he had engaged in premarital sex. "I have even participated in a three way, Father, and am so ashamed."

Well, Father Jake's pecker instantly began to rise. He quickly lifted his robe, applied a generous amount of Lucy's Lube and told his charge, "Say t-t-t-th-th-th-three H-H-H-Ha-Hai-Hail M-M-M-M-M-Maaaaaaaa-rrryyyyyyyysssss!"

Thankful but confused over the priest's heightened state of excitement, the young man asked, "Will I be absolved, Father?"

Panting and heavy breathing preceded the holy man's reply: "Oooooh, y-y-y-yeeeeeessssssssss!! Oooooh....."

Before you know it, miracles of miracles, Father Jake was coming in quarts! That lube will do it every time.

"What a heavenly, holy gift it is," sighed the Father, totally spent and unable to hear any more confessions that Saturday.

3

Some of my popular items here at the store are the whips in the leather section. In fact, I have a regular customer who is quite happy with creating the sound of a cracking whip. She brings to mind an amusing story.

She is known as Wicked Whipping Edwina. There is a massage parlor in town called "The Hot Hands" of which she has been the owner for some time. A varied clientele has come to her place for a nice --- ahhm! --- *massage*: men and women, old and young, singles, married, swingers --- you name it! The parlor's main attraction has been none other than Edwina herself. She is known far and wide for her specialty in leather, with her main feature being her whip. She and that whip of hers have always been big hits. People have come from everywhere just to take advantage of some of her exquisite whippings. [*Whoosh*! I can just hear her whipping away in my mind!]

Her "special treatment" consists of having her clientele beg her to whip them. And you'd be surprised who has come in for these kinky sessions: a prominent bank manager, a noted local politician and, last but not least, the leader of a local chapter of "The Christian Moral Values Association." Hmm…, it looks like we all have some type of skeletons in our closets, huh?

One evening a fine upstanding individual arrived

at the usual time at "The Hot Hands" for his regular appointment. "Glory be!" he shouted to the receptionist, raising his hands in worshipful praise. "Let us rejoice in this wonderful day that the Lord has made!" Leaning over the desk and grinning, he added, "I'll have my usual, please." The receptionist chuckled and directed him to room number 9.

The hallowed leader made himself comfortable in the designated room and moments later, in walked none other than Edwina herself. She was scantily dressed in lace panties, an ample latex bra and shiny black leather boots. She eyed her customer with contempt and took charge in no time. "Strip off those disgusting clothes and get your fat ass up on that table, you holier-than-thou son of a bitch!"

The sanctimonious man of the God of all that's good and pure obeyed without flinching, making himself buck naked in seconds. He spread himself flat on the table, arching slightly to make his ass cheeks stick up in the air. Before you know it Edwina was whipping away! With each noisy stroke of her trusty lash, she coaxed him along as part of her special turn-on. She had him repeat several phrases, punctuating each sentence with a firm whipping against his ever-reddening buttocks.

"Repeat after me, you pious scumbag: 'Thank you, Mister President!'...[*whoosh*!]... 'Thank you, almighty commander in chief!...[*swack*!]... 'I love your wall!'... [*smack*!]... 'It's going up!'...[*crack*!]... 'It's going to be a big wall!'....[*blister*!] 'Build it tall!'...[*bruise*!] 'Build it wide!'...[*swish-swash-injure-pain*!]..."

At the point he was about to shoot his load, the thoroughly beaten and bruised man yelled, "Oh, thank you, Jesus! Thanks and praise be to you, my Savior, for this glorious whipping! It's precisely the thing I desire and deserve! Thank you, dear Lord, for supplying ALL my needs so thoroughly, allowing my cup to runneth over..." He arose from the table, still raising his hands in worship and jabbering away. His ass was a beet red. Mistress Edwina, the confirmed artist that she is, had even managed to whip a fairly large cross over one of his butt cheeks.

I guess they don't call her Wicked Whipping Edwina for nothing!

4

I notice over here that we a large selection of dildos, complete with cocks and balls attached, too. They're all very popular and sell out pretty fast.

This brings to mind the story about some of our regular clientele. They are what I call the Double Headed Dildo Threesome. Their names are Janice, Jason and Jeffery. All three come from the upper echelon of society. At least that's what they want us to believe. But when those three get together, they all live completely different lives.

Believe me, it is a sight to see. All of them love to play roles. Jeffery drinks, gets drunk and parades around like a know-it-all and a bragging king. Janice, while using her dildo, acts like the Queen of Egypt. Jason dresses in women's underclothes: panties and bra, topped off with a wig.

They have one thing in common: they all love to take turns getting it up the ass. When they really get going, they are wild.

"Yes, my slave, worship your Queen of the Nile," Janice sighs as she places it up Jason's ass.

"Oh, dearie! Kiss me, my love, fuck me!" cries Jason. Jeffery goes into his British routine. "By Jove, you're all looking *rah-ther* horny. I'd love a bit of a shag meself."

Getting blindly drunk he dances around, then grabs their double-headed dildo. "Pardon me, old chaps, but please don't hog this lovely long tally-wacker! Let me have it up the ol' arse, my dear."

Janice takes it, shoves up his and maneuvers it up hers. She grabs her whip, wraps a large feather boa around her shoulders and waves both of them menacingly around him. "Take this, you slut of a drunken servant! Get down on all fours and let me shove it into you with my royal hands."

For their grand finale they form a pyramid, getting on top of one other. They bring out another double-headed dildo and shove it into each other, humping away.

It looks like those double-headed dildos satisfy even the most regal of assholes.

5

We have other special goodies here in the store. Some are designed to boost the ol' cock, dick or pecker. You probably have heard about some of them, such as Spanish Fly and other aphrodisiacs.

This little bottle I am holding here in my hand really does the trick. It packs a powerful wallop! It has helped many a man with getting his ol' boner up. There have been many men who have testified to this *bottle of the hard-on*.

It brings to mind a couple of our customers who have tried it. One particular involved a young man named Shawn and a young lady, Cindy. They were both eighteen. This was their first time ever, for they were both virgins. Can you imagine that?

One day Shawn, as all young males who have sex on their minds but are still a little shy, decided to visit our store without telling Cindy or anyone else. He walked in, looked rather excited and a little nervous about coming into a sex store. I tried to put his mind at ease.

"May I help you?"

"Yes, I would love to go on my first date, and I'm planning to have my very first sexual encounter. I want to be nice, hot and ready."

I could tell that he was all excited about having his first lay. He looked around and was drawn to Paul's Power Pecker Pills. "I'd love to buy a bottle of this, if I may. I am eager to please my date. I'm very hung, you know, at least that's what others have said. The guys in gym class kid me about it all the time in the showers."

I told him that since this was his first time taking these pills, he must carefully follow the instructions. He just stood there and laughed "I'll be OK. I can handle anything, I'm no pussy!" I smiled and said nothing to him.

Well, that night Shawn took Cindy out to the movies. Before the show started she told him that she had to use the bathroom to freshen up a bit. While she was gone, Shawn very quickly brought out his bottle of pills and took one. Thinking for a moment, he said to himself, "Aw, shit, I'll take two!" He washed them down with a Coke.

Cindy returned and sat down. "The timing is right," he thought, "I'll just make my move now." He placed his arm around her and they both cuddled up to each other. Before you know it he noticed that he was getting aroused and that young cock of his was beginning to rise. It was really quite embarrassing to him. He began to really get hard and it even tore through his pants. In no time the thing was sticking out from his pants. He even tried to adjust his zipper, but his member was too large and bulging. Poor little Shawn. [Little? I mean big, huge, giant-headed Shawn!]

Cindy even noticed it and was blushing beet red. Moments later, in walked an usher. He aimed his flashlight in Shawn's direction and saw his large, protruding appendage.

"Hey, you!" the usher yelled. "Put that damn dick away and pull up your pants, or I'll arrest you for lewd conduct."

He tried and tried, even attempting to hide it with his bag of popcorn, but it was no use. That cock of his kept getting harder and harder. He grabbed Cindy's hand, they got quickly got up and hurried out of the theater. Shawn struggled to cover up his boner with his jacket, but alas, he had grown bigger, another full two inches!

The next day he went to school, but it was still larger than ever. He went to the washroom, pulled out the bottle and looked at the information on the label. "Let's see here: it says to only take one. Oh, and in fine print there's a warning: just a single dose will apparently keep you hard for four hours. Taking more can lead to severe hardness and the user may even suffer from an enlarged penis."

For the remainder of that day the kids in school laughed their heads off. He became known as "The Big Dicked Kid."

It looks like that little bottle of pecker power will do *big things* every time!

6

There was one other encounter with this wondrous bottle of penis power. This heavenly pecker-riser story takes place in a nuns' convent. It's about the secret life of Sister Beatrice.

She was a loved by all. She was even in line to be the new Mother Superior. All was blessed and going well for her, but no one knew her other side. She had kept it secret for quite some time. I learned about it as part of my usual routine at the store.

One day a man by the name of Mike came in and told me that he was looking for an extra pick-me-up in the cock. He had a hard time getting it up. I asked what the problem was. Mike shared with me that *he* was actually a *she* and was living as a nun, calling *her*self Sister Beatrice. His [or hers] only earthly joy was that of getting hard and having fantasies of getting it on with the other sisters.

She would often go into the shower and later that evening would have a nocturnal emission. I showed the bottle of Paul's Power Pecker Pills to him [her] and warned that he [she] must be careful of how much to take. I assured him [her] that if he [she] was doing the Lord's work, it would be OK.

Mike paid for it and left the store. That night, he became Sister Beatrice and took one, then another, and asked the Lord for a double blessing. The sisters noticed that evening that something was on the rise: *her* dick, of all things! How embarrassing this was.

Our heavenly sister had a huge hard-on. She ran and hid under her covers, pretending to be fast asleep.

A couple of the sisters noticed a large something sticking up like a hill from her bedsheets. This looked rather strange to them. One of them tiptoed over, raised the sheet and shrieked, "Good God! Sweet Sister Beatrice has a penis. She is a he, not a she!"

Sister Beatrice awoke and saw them standing beside her bed. She needed to explain herself, and fast! She was taken to the Mother Superior to confess her dastardly, sinful deed. Poor Sister Beatrice would have faced dismissal from the convent had it not been for a small miracle at the last minute.

The Mother Superior was a woman of great wisdom, understanding and creativity. Not only did she not consider forcing Sister Beatrice to leave, but had a brilliant alternative. "Since your --- ahem! --- male appendage (she arched her eyebrow as she emphasized the word!) never seems to want to go down, I have decided to place you as head of our choir. You shall use your heavenly *gift* as a baton."

Sister Beatrice was kept in the convent and excelled as choir director. Even today the nuns refer to her fleshy baton as "The Blessed Pecker of Consumption." Her fame has spread throughout all of Christendom.

Hmm…, it looks like Paul's Power Pecker Pills have even more blessed wonderworking power than meets the eye!

7

As I go through my inventory I notice a very popular item, especially with the ladies. Most women just love them. They give them a sexy and more appealing look. They draw the men and cause guys to chase after them.

Let me just say: there is nothing like a nice pair of Tina's Titillating Titties! They fit nicely, shivering and shaking just like real ones. You either place them in your bra or attach them to your breast area. They're just like having real tits. People from all walks of life use them: ladies, girls, cross dressers, transvestites, transgender women --- in short, anyone who wants to wear boobs! The also come with real nipples which, if rubbed, will become fully erect and give you that turned-on feeling.

I know of many women who tell me that they feel like a million bucks with these bouncy, shaky tits. Schoolgirls who were formerly flat-chested achieve a new lease on life, thanks to Tina's Titillating Titties.

There were two high school girls named Tracy and Trisha who became very popular, especially among horny young men. Boys followed them everywhere, longing to get their hands, mouths and tongues on those tits. One of them was Bob. He especially loved to grab a hold of them and squish away. It really got his good ol' pecker up and a-goin'. His buddy, an equally horny young guy named Matthew, bragged to other guys in school, "Hey man, you should grab yourself a handful of Tracy's and Trisha's boobs. What hot chicks they are!"

The two girls always had trouble with shooing the horndogs away. They had to smack many a boy. Some even went home with red and bruised faces, they had been slapped so hard. Those breasts were so realistic, they made all the male students' hormones work overtime. Thanks to those surgical silicone teardrop tits the lives of Tracy and Trisha were transformed.

Don't forget our special this week only: Two Boobs For The Price Of One. I wish you happy squeezing!

8

As I browse through my assortment of delectable goodies I have here our delightful, lovely, luscious cucumber cunts. These tongue-tantalizing cunts contain the cool, refreshing taste of cucumbers. They will tingle and satisfy your taste buds.

That brings to mind a gentleman whom I refer to as Fellatio Joe. He was something else! He'd stick his tongue into whatever he could get it into. You might say he had an oral fixation. He would often daydream about giving oral service. At times he paraded around talking to himself. He would go into his Shakespearean routine, for he was also a man of the stage:

"Ah!
To tongue or not to tongue?
That is the licking question.
Whether 'tis nobler to
fellatio or cunnilingus,
that is the oral dilemma!"

Going back to his constant daydreaming, he continued pondering, "Let's see, whose cunt, ass or cock shall I invade with this princely tongue?"

Besides his oral fixation, Joe had another fascinating hobby: he loved to drink to excess. When he got drunk he stuck his tongue in all the wrong places. One day he happened to come upon a wall socket. Lo and behold, he began to stick his eager tongue in it. He got knocked on his ass giving oral sex to electricity. One hundred twenty volts coursed through his trembling body and he got the shock of his life. Needless to say, he didn't survive long enough to tell us what a tongue-tingling time he had experienced.

Alas, poor Fellatio Joe, I knew you well.

So dear friends, let this be a lesson to you: always be careful where you place your tongue. It can be quite shocking --- heh-heh-heh!

I don't want to forget to mention our fine assortment of condoms. We specialize in French ticklers. They will give you a spine-tingling, spike-teasing sensation.

This reminds me of a story I like to call "The Midnight Ride of the French Tickler." I have had a lot of interesting people come through these doors, but one of them really sticks out! [Get it?] One day a middle aged man in his early forties approached my counter.

"Hello. Excuse me, but where are your condoms?"

"They're over there on the ass-cheek tray."

"Oh, thank you ever so much. I'm looking for a special one."

He began browsing through them and found one he took a real fancy to. "Ah, I found it! This French tickler. How many of these do you have?"

I brought out a box of them. He quickly grabbed a dozen, paid for them and gushed, "I just love these. They really give me a good ride." The last thing I remember him saying as he exited the store was, "The Midnight French Tickler Rides Again!"

I subsequently learned that this gentleman had quite an imagination with regard to his sexual prowess. When he arrived at a house of pleasure for his evening lay he rang the bell outside. The proprietor opened the door and beheld a man dressed in a rather strange outfit: black cape, a powdered wig and a three cornered hat. He stormed in, dropped his pants, ran around the room with his erect member sticking out and loudly proclaimed, "It's me, the Midnight Rider of the French Tickler. Let me saddle my horse and watch for my signal: one screw by land, two fucks by sea!"

He soon had his French tickler firmly in place and ready to go. "The British may be coming, the British may be coming!" he cried. "But believe me, this rider is about to come right now!"

His fame spread wherever he went. That is, however, until one night when he was caught prancing around in a public park and showed his tickler to the wrong person: it was the wife of the local chief of police. Such a shame: the French Tickler will ride no more!

In my world of the obscene and being naughty there is nothing like the sucking, puckering power of a nice blowjob. Oh! Look what we have here: it's a pair of Linda's Vibrating Tongue-tingling lips.

For all you men out there, the lips can either be placed on the tip of the head of your cock or the bottom of your shaft. Simply turn on the vibrating lips and you will get the most succulent experience ever.

These lips are available in an array colors: pink, yellow, orange, light blue and rainbow. You will find that these lips come in quite handy, especially when you have no real lips to turn to.

This reminds me of a story of a man who was in such a predicament. Leroy was his name. He had been married at one time, but his wife had left him. He was caught giving too much lip service. You know what I mean? He was such a little horny toad. He even liked to swing the other way, looking for willing men, too.

Leroy was an older man in his mid-sixties, but he just couldn't find the right kind of lips. He was rather picky as to what pair of lips he wanted. That's why he finally chose to come into our store. Leroy walked in and looked around. His eyes opened wide and sparkled with excitement.

"Oh wow! Big fucking lips! I'd love to have one of these pairs wrapped around my head. I can just imagine a nice pair of them going down on my shaft!"

He noticed a pair that stood out to him. "This one here is battery operated," I explained to him, "and it vibrates."

"Holy shit! These lips are just the right ones for my pecker!" He bought the lips, went home and tried them on. They had a switch which activated the vibrator. He placed them on the head of his cock and let it rip.

"Oh fuck!" he cried with ecstasy. "This is just like getting the real thing: a nice hot blowjob." As he enjoyed the pleasurable sensation the vibrating lips gave him, Leroy removed his glasses and threw them on the floor, forgetting that he was as blind as a bat without them. He fiddled around with the controls, trying to switch the lips off, but everything was a blur. "Oh well," he shrugged, "I don't have to worry. I'll just walk around with it still attached until I can find my damn glasses."

He remembered that he hadn't taken a bath all day. He still tried to unsnap the lips, but they would not come off. His pecker got harder and harder, but this was quite usual for him anyway, so he just drew the bath water and decided to jump in, lips attached and all.

"Lord have mercy," he screeched, "these goddamn things are short-circuiting in this bath water!" Leroy got the biggest, most shocking blowjob ever He shot his load fifty times in the following hour. It was most satisfying, but he was totally wasted and thought it best to check himself into the hospital for a full evaluation. The funny thing was (and the doctors and nurses surely got a good laugh out of it): he never did find his glasses and was forced to keep the vibrator lips locked around his dick. He was diagnosed with orgasmic tremors.

"I'm afraid your lip-service sucking days are over, my dear sir," the attending doctor informed him.

Poor Leroy!

There is another section of my store that I have not even touched on yet. It's a world of chains, whips, slings and pain.It's amazing to me that people actually get off on that! Oh, by the way, there goes a customer of mine! He is very into that type of scene. He is known for his "House of Pain with Pleasure."

That reminds me of his story. I call his home "Ted's Torture Chamber." When you enter into his bedroom, it's one of forbidden darkness. All the accessories of pain-inducing sexual fulfillment are there for the taking. Strangely, Ted is known as a fine upstanding citizen in the community. He works as a judge and loves to dress in women's undergarments. I call him "Ted the Spanking-Wanking Judge."

He has some regular friends who get together for some "painstaking" fun. One of them is Jason who loves to dress as an Indian chief. He likes to be chained, whipped and spanked.

Another participant is Hank. He is a professor of Egyptology. When he is present in the chamber, he loves to give orders to others, handcuff them and force them into one of Ted's slings. He enjoys dishing out humiliation. He wears his Pharaoh costume and makes all others his slaves.

What a group they all make! A slinging, butt-smacking, whacking, pain-giving trio. It's a sight to behold. I can just imagine them all going at it. Old Judge Ted stands at the door in his female underclothing and wig, seductively saying, "Hi, darlings. Welcome to my chamber of pain. Are you ready, my sweeties?" His smile turns into an evil smirk as he cracks his whip. "Come on, you scum bags," he snarls. "Get going already!"

Jason the Indian glances around and murmurs, "Mmm…, me like 'em red ass, give it to me heap big!" I guess they don't call him "Chief Pain in the Ass" for nothing.

The Pharaoh brings out his handcuffs and demands, "Bow down to me, all you worthless slave turds. Lick my royal boots and kiss my royal *High-n-ass*! I am your beating, bruising King of the Nile. Down on your knees, you worthless bitches! Service my cock while I tie you inside my sling!"

Well, word spread far and wide about his place. Believe it or not, half of the town's police force, high profile attorneys plus leaders of local Girl and Boy Scout troops even joined in the fun. What wild activity goes on nonstop in that judge's torture chamber!

For those of you who would love something nice stuck up your ass, try our new Buddy's Butt Plug. There's nothing like its bouncy, rubbery resilience up the butt. They're just right for those who like to get fucked when there's no cock around.

There was this customer whose story I must share with you.   He was Bob the Butt-Plugin' Man. Whenever he used his butt plug he also told some one liners, for he had been at one time an old vaudeville comedian.

"Why did the rubber go flying across the room? It was pissed off." [*yuck-yuck*] "For those of you out there who love sports, what do you get when you have two cocks and one ball? A double header!" [*horselaughs*] "What did one asshole say to the other asshole? Why the hell are we hanging around with these two bums?" [*a laugh riot!*]

One day, something went awry as he was using his butt plug. He was carrying on with his usual jokes: "What did one dick say to the other dick? It's getting too hard for me to laugh!" [*a few chuckles*] and such like. When he was done telling his jokes he rushed back to his dressing room. He sat at a vanity table where he had spread out various jars of creams and ointments as well as a few food items to snack on. Staring at himself in the mirror as he wiped some grease paint off his face, he reached for a small container which he thought was lubricant. In fact, he had accidentally grabbed a jar of cheese spread for crackers and bread, using it to slip his butt plug up his ass. When it felt snug he sat on it and rode it like a horse. "Giddayup there," he shouted, "the Lone Butt Plugger rides again!"

In his excitement, he went to feel his plug and to his horror discovered that it had completely disappeared. It had slipped all the way up inside his ass. He panicked and rushed to the closest hospital. Inside the emergency room he burst into tears.

"Doctor," he cried, "my Buddy's Butt Plug slipped too far up my ass. I can't get it out. What do I do?"

The doctor took his penlight, aimed it and said, "Open up so I can see in there." Bending down and aiming the light strategically at his butthole, he gagged. "Whew!" he gasped, looking away and pinching his nostrils. "Your shit sure does stink. I'll have to explore a bit more in detail. Just give me a chance to catch my breath!" Slipping on a pair of rubber gloves the doctor performed a routine rectal exam, sticking his hand in quite a bit farther than normal.

"What the hell's going on, Doc?" Bob asked, feeling the physician's fingers wiggling inside him. "Are you trying to pull my butt plug out?"

The doctor smiled benignly and replied, "Of course I am, my friend, but first I'll have to pull out that pesky rat that's jumped in after the cheese."

So, boys and girls, the moral of this story is: always be careful what you stick up there!

There is another popular treat that our clients literally eat up: Eddie's Edible Undies. Everyone just loves their luscious, yummy flavors: Hot Chocolate, Lemon-Lime, Apple Pie and, for a real hot sensation, Chili Peppers! The girls especially love to get their asses munched on.

There was this one man in particular who loved to eat on ladies' undies. John was his name. He would go to our store and buy up a dozen or more of them. I heard tell of something happening to him. Well, the scuttlebutt is that he came home one day and emptied several whole bags full of them. John had been recently divorced and pretended to be eating away on his wife's ass.

"Mmm…," he purred. "I can sure munch on a nice ass right now. Let's see…, I'll start out with some of that yummy Apple Pie, then I'll try a little of that Lemon-Lime."

He just pigged out on those undies! His only problem this time was that he became very greedy, wanting more and more. He was almost finished going through a dozen of them. However, he was about to get an unexpected *hot* surprise, you might say. Someone [I don't know who] quite by accident mislabeled one of the packages of undies. The tag read *Hot Chocolate*.

"Wow!" John exclaimed. "That looks real yummy. Imagine eating a nice hot chocolate ass!" He ripped it open and munched away. Immediately his mouth felt like it was on fire. "Holy Shit! What kind of chocolate was *that*?" He examined the package closely and noticed that the color was more reddish than brown.

"Oh, no! It must be those hot Chili Peppers." He gulped and added, "And I just polished off a half dozen of them!"

He raced around the room like his tail was on fire. He ran out on his back porch and spotted a bottle on a table. The label was facing away from him, but he supposed it was only water. He drank it quickly. Feeling the liquid splash against his tongue, he gasped in terror. He looked at the bottle and was shocked to read the letters printed on the label: KEROSENE. He spit it all out and coughed uncontrollably, almost gagging.

Poor ol' John. Sometimes it's not wise to have too much of a good thing.

14

I see that I have here one of our popular novelties. It's a Cock and Balls Wall Light. It looks rather hung, don't you think? Not only can you use it for hot sex, but it can be used as a guiding light for your bedroom.

This ample-sized wanking tool will give you many of hours of fucking pleasure. The mighty pecker also comes with some nice large hanging balls. You simply squeeze them and they let out a moan, followed by a flickering red-pinkish sparkle.

No other lovely prick will light up your bedroom quite like it. It will give you oodles of ball-busting fun.

You know, there was a little man who just loved to use this product. He has asked for anonymity, so I shall merely refer to him as Naughty Nathan and tell you that he lived along the shores of New England.

Nathan was well liked by others in the community. Little did any of his fellow citizens or neighbors know that he had what I like to call a saucy secret life. Simply put: he loved sticking his cock and balls into anywhere he found a hole. Aside from this, he had a rather comical fetish. He enjoyed dressing up as a pirate and showing off, shall we say, his *gift*. He lured potential sex partners into the lighthouse located on his property and stunned them by displaying his Cock and Balls Wall Light.

Whenever he invited "dates" over, he went into his exaggerated pirate voice imitation and performed a routine he had rehearsed. "Ahoy there, me matey! I'm Captain Long Dong Pecker." If more than one unsuspecting soul showed up, he'd say heartily, "Welcome aboard my ship, me buckos. Where and when shalt I fuck ye?"

He lurked in the shadows and gave his tingling balls on the wall clock a good squeeze. Everyone would hear a moan, followed by his hearty laughter. "Batten down the hatches!" he loudly proclaimed. "Watch out, here it comes!"

He then whipped out the Cock and Balls Wall Light. "Would you care to have a sword fight?" He stuck it out right in front of his victim. "Here, grab thou mine cock and me balls, me matey!" he cried. When the individual did, it let out its usual moan, followed by its flickering and twinkling red-pinkish light.

"I'm your Captain now," he bellowed. "I run this fucking ship!" He issued forth some stern commands. "Follow me to my cabin, you flirty wench, and don't resist!"

He slammed the door shut and yelled. "Here, my lovely lady, is your reward: my nice thick hard cock with hanging balls. Come, let your Captain shove it up your pirate's cove!" He issued forth an evil laugh and added, "Grab me balls!" He moaned and the light engulfed his bedroom. It was a sight to behold.

Rumors spread regarding that strange lighthouse in town, especially among the lovely ladies. They couldn't wait to see and try out that cock and balls contraption for themselves. His place was known as "Captain Long Dong's Groaning Pecker of Guiding Light."

Let's set sail, and away we go!

As I go through the store I do want to mention Tina's other products. There is one in particular that I'm sure you will enjoy and want to have. It's for those of you who love tea as well as tits: it's Tina's Titty Tea Set. It is simply elegant and makes a lovely set of tits for use around the house.

These tea cups, the tea pot and tea tray are all sculpted in the shape of titillating tits. Imagine, drinking your favorite tea in an actual breast form! They all come complete with nice hardened nipples, too.

There was this older male couple who have visited here and fell in love this titty tea set. Their names are Bob Rothschild and Andrew Devonshire. Both originally hailed from London, England, but now lived in an exclusive area of Beverly Hills, California. They just loved to have their afternoon tea every time with the tea set.

"Oh, Bob darling!" Andrew peeped. "I say, it's high time for our tea."

"Ooh, you're so right, love!" his prissy partner said. "Don't forget to bring out that lovely Tina's Titty Tea Set!"

"Quite-quite, my sweet!" the mincing Andrew responded. "There's simply nothing like a nice spot of tea and a tit, say what?!"

"Hear, hear, my pet! Like I always say, there is nothing like the nice fresh, piping hot taste of tea in a tit." Moments later, Bob brings out his tea set. "Here we go, my dear. I'll do the pouring."

"My word!" cried Andrew. "The nice bit of tea is pouring right through the old hard nipple. Absolutely smashing!"

"By Jove, you're right, Andy!" exclaimed Bob. "I simply love the breast forms on the tray as well. They have a squishy touch --- just the way a tit should be." Covering his mouth to stifle a little giggle, he added, "Speaking of tits, dear boy, I can go for a nice nipple play myself right now."

"Rah-*ther*!" Andrew replied excitedly.

"If you have no objection, Andy dear, I'll even pour a little tea on *your* tit, just to spice things up a bit."

"Don't you dare!" the frightened man screamed. "You'll burn me bloody nipple!" Catching his breath, he added, "I know we've spoken often about hot tits, but such an idea is out of the question."

Bob assumed a haughty air. "Pish and tish!" he barked. "That means you won't be able to give any more milk, you frustrated old maid. Big deal!

"How dare you insult my nipple!" the other man declared, incensed. "I'll have you know that mine are of among the hardest and most erect that you'll find anywhere, you mean old maid!"

Bob tried to calm Andy down. "Now, now! Let us tired queens behave ourselves before our tea gets too cold!"

Andrew smiled and replied, "Quite right, my love.

I say, let's call a truce and enjoy our nice titillating cups of tea. Would you also care for a cucumber sandwich or some clotted cream, Snookie Ookums?"

Well, it looks like Tina's Titty Tea Set does it again! Both of these tea drinking dilettantes broke into an impromptu joyous song:

Tea for two,
and I love you.
Tits for two,
for me and you!

"There's nothing a nice healthy sip from a tit, don't you agree, Bob?" Andrew asked, tittering. "My word, I could use a good shag this very moment!" They continued laughing and singing the afternoon away.

16

Looking through the store here, I do love all the assortments of yummy edibles. One of my favorite flavors is vanilla. There is an edible I must recommend that you try: Virginia's Vanilla Vaginas. They're a real taste sensation especially if you are throwing a party.

There was this one woman whose story I simply must share with you. Her name was Tammy Shaw and she lived in the Victorian Mansions section of Los Angeles, California. She had this fixation on the movie *Gone With The Wind* and she loved playing the role of Scarlet O'Hara. She would even wear the same type of dresses from that era. When she had her tea or coffee gatherings, she was in full Southern belle attire, wearing a party dress from those days.

I do recall one of the ladies telling me all about those parties. According to her, Tammy would greet the ladies. "Why, hello there, all you girls! Thank y'all for comin'. Would y'all care for some li'l ol' tea or coffee?"

The girls gave her their orders while they were gabbing away. Tammy went into her pitch for the vanilla vaginas.

"I have something delicious to share with you ladies. I have this lovely taste treat which has a sweet yummy flavor. They're such a big hit with the boys." She summoned her maid to go in the kitchen and a sterling plate was brought out. "I have here some delectable goodies," she continued excitedly. "I bought them over at 'Fifi's Erotic Boutique.'"

All the girls oohed and aahed in surprise. "They're called Virginia's Vanilla Vaginas," Tammy exclaimed. She began to brag about men she had invited over to try them while the ladies present just sat amazed, giggling demurely and laughing out loud at times.

"Well, sir," she went on, "there was one recent gentlemen caller named Beauregard. When I wanted him to get into, you know, *the mood*, I just brought out one of them li'l ol' vaginas. Honey child, y'all never saw a man get so red in the face like he did! I told him to try one and he just loved it. I declare, he was just wantin' more and more."

The ladies leaned forward with their mouths agape. "What happened then?" they asked, barely able to control their curiosity and expectation.

"Well," she began, "he looked over at me and I raised my skirt just an itty bit. He cried, 'I'd like to have some that thar real stuff! Y'know, that thar genuine one down there between your pretty li'l legs.'"

The ladies burst out laughing. "Why, before y'all know," Tammy continued, "li'l ol' Beauregard was actin' like a wild man. We were both makin' love in my soft silky bed."

I heard tell that one girl asked, "Was he worth it?"

"He sure enough was, darlin'!" Tammy replied saucily. "That gorgeous pecker of his was as big as a donkey's dingle-dangle."

The assembled ladies exchanged knowing glances with one another and were so impressed that it caused each of them to come here and buy some for their boyfriends, too!

I always say that there's nothin' like the good ol' southern comfort of a vanilla vagina!

It is also a good idea to have fun and always enjoy your sex. That brings me to some of our fabulous items. Let me introduce you to Dolly's Inflatable Dolls. They come in male or female versions.

I recall an incident which recently took place. There were two young boys in their early twenties. They were sort of wise-ass kids. I even happened to overhear them talking when they recently visited the store:

"Hey Billy!"

"Yeah, Jason! Whadya want?"

"Take a look at these blow-up dolls. I'd love to have *this* nice girl give me some head."

"Aww, your dick is so small it wouldn't even fit in her."

"Why, ya probably never got yerself a piece o' ass before either!"

"Hey! I got me a cool idea. Let's buy a chick for each of us."

"Whad're we gonna to do, fuck 'em?"

They both laughed and agreed to buy the dolls just for the fun of it. When I handed them the boxes, they took a brief look at the information written alongside the brand name and logo.

"Look, man!" Billy exclaimed. "It says here that this chick comes with a vibrating vagina, nice hard nipples and a tight ass."

"Wow!" responded Jason, totally in awe. "A pussy

that shakes, erect nipples and a snug asshole! I always wanted to do it to a chick up the ass, dude."

Billy nodded in agreement and they decided to go over to Jason's apartment. When they arrived they hurriedly opened the boxes and began blowing up the dolls. In no time flat they were at it. Billy proceeded to stick his --- uhmm! --- *big hammer* into the girl doll's vagina.

"Oh, cool!" he purred contentedly. "This feels so fuckin' good --- just like a real nice warm cunt, and it fuckin' vibrates to boot!"

Jason was all excited, as young men are apt to be, took his doll and stuck his own member into its ass. 'This is sure-shit fuckin' fantastic!" he cried. "Ain't nothin' like a hot ass, nice and tight, that's for sure!"

They had both been going at it hot and heavy for quite a while when suddenly they noticed something was terribly amiss.

"Hey, Billy! Damn it, somethin's wrong. I can't get my dick out o' this doll. It's fuckin' stuck and feels like it's swollen or somethin' worse."

Jason nodded in his friend's direction and had a worried look on his face. "Y'know, it's the same here with me. My prick is stuck up her ass and I can't get it out. I've been pullin' and pullin', but nothin' happens."

Jason was in terrific pain, but with his pecker still stuck up the girl doll's ass managed to limp over to when they'd throw the packing boxes off to one side in the bedroom. "Holy shit, man! Look what the fuck it says: 'Overuse of this product can cause unwanted swelling of the sex organ.' Oh, fuck!"

You'll forgive me for laughing, dear friends. It just tickles me to think about how long it took those poor boys to cut those dolls loose from their peckers. I guess they got their just deserves and both learned a --- ***ahem*** ---- *hard* lesson. Always be careful what you poke with your pecker!

18

There is nothing like special wear when it comes to the ladies. I recommend here at the store Linda Lace's Lovely Lingerie. It's great for your panties, bras and the sexy see-through nightgowns. They come in pastel pink, light blue and, most delicious of all, white with sparkles.

There was a lovely lady who is a customer of ours. She comes in from time to time. Let me tell you her story. People called her Loveable Lucy Lou. She worked as a striptease dancer at "The Erotic Fantasy," a gentlemen's club here in town. Evenings there were jammed-packed with wild, horny, crazy men. They came from far and wide, mainly just to see Lucy Lou perform in her special lingerie. Her male admirers included police officers, lawyers and those serving in the military.

When she hit the stage all eyes were on her. She was introduced and then slowly stripped off her clothes until she was down to her sexy silky panties and bra. The men loved to hear her make purring sounds like a cat. During her show she sang in a sultry manner akin to Mae West:

"Why don't you
come up to my room
and see me sometime,
big boy?
And I do mean big,

if ya get my drift!
Lemme see those
hot packages of yours, boys."

Lucy Lou was down to her skimpy panties and waving all her hot stuff right in front of their noses. She approached some of the men at their tables, slowly pulled on the elastic band around her waist, upon which the excited crowd eagerly stuffed tens and twenties into her waiting panties.

Yesiree! Lucy Lou became the talk of the town and word about her spread across several continents. She got the biggest surprise of her life one night when a handsome sailor boy proposed to her. Besides being virile and extremely good looking, he was also "gifted" in other ways, something to which Lucy Lou's attention was undoubtedly drawn.

Well, wonders of wonders: she accepted his generous proposal and they were married at once. Their honeymoon took a different kind of twist. After checking into a luxurious hotel suite, Charlie (for that was her new husband's name) announced that he wanted to take a quick shower. She prepared for bed and waited patiently until he came out of the bathroom.

"Close your eyes, dearest," he shouted after turning off the water. "I have something wonderful to show you." She became excited at the prospect of seeing him in all his glory, for she knew that he was super well-endowed.

"I have them closed, my love," she responded, arranging herself under the covers and propping up the pillow, "and I can hardly wait to see what wonders you have to show me."

A minute or two passed, then he flung open the bathroom door, pranced out and stood at the foot of the bed. "Open your eyes and behold," Charlie said. She obeyed and upon catching sight of him as he playfully danced around in see-through nightgown, she smiled broadly.

"I detect a pair of lace panties and a bra underneath that nightgown, sweetie," she cooed. "Am I right?"

He slipped off the nightgown and revealed them to her exactly as she had described. They both laughed with glee. "As you can see," he proclaimed, "I am a lover of Linda Lace's Lingerie, too. I hope you don't mind, my pet."

Not only was she not offended, she led him in a chorus of a song which was a favorite of both of theirs:

"Anchors away,
my boy,
Anchors away."

That just goes to show you that even some of those seafaring salty dogs also love to wear Linda Lace's Lingerie!

19

I did mention earlier during this tour of our store that we have the Cock in the Clock. We can special order it for you if you wish.

There was a gentleman who bought one recently. He collects rare sex toys and novelties. His name is Professor Erich von Grossenburger. He graduated from Humboldt University in Berlin, majoring in sexology and human development. He works as a therapist and helps patients with their sexual problems. He is in his late fifties and has long blond frizzed-out hair. He kind of reminds me of someone who sticks his finger in a wall socket and gets the shock of his life.

I can recall the day he came in. He browsed around the store and looked like he was getting rather turned on by what he was seeing. "*Ach du lieber*," he cried in his native German, "vaht a big dildo *das ist*! It gives me a pain in *meine Arsche* just to see it."

He then looked at the wall display and declared with excitement. "*Gott im Himmel*, how *wunderbar* zis clock looks." I assured him that this was no ordinary clock, but rather *Cock* in the Clock. I went on to explain to him that when it strikes at the top of each hour, a huge surprise pops out. "*Ach, ja!*" he said, nodding vigorously. "*Wir kommen* at zis moment almost to the top of ze hour, *Liebling*."

He could barely contain his enthusiasm and

curiosity, squirming and gyrating in a weird way. As the second hand reached the 12-mark on the clock face, the cock popped out and squirted its *créme de la cum*!

"*Menschenskind*, vaht a big *spritz* zaht *ist*!" the doctor yelled, totally losing his ordinarily professional demeanor. "*Das ist* really *ein* gusher of a *spritz*." Lowering his voice, he asked, "I vahnt to have one of zeez clocks for *mein* office. I think it vill help ze patients *mit* sexual problems to over*kommen* all zose shtupid hangups zey *haben.* I love it and I think *mein* clients will love it, too!"

He hastily paid for it and wanted to grab the display clock off the wall immediately, determined to carry it under his arm out of the store and not even bother with a bag. I told him that it was the only one I had at that time and that I would have to order one especially for him. He was upset, but cooperated.

In two weeks' time he received the package from my retailer. I have since heard that his consultation office has become quite a hit in this town, and his business is brisker than ever. "Ach, *mein* patients just love zat vunderful boner as it happens every hour. In fact, I charge ze crazies even more because everybody vants *zu sh*tay longer in *mein* office to see it."

As Professor von Grossenburger often asks, "Care for some *cremé de la cum* in your coffee?!"

20

For those of you who like to punish someone for being a little naughty I recommend Patty's Paddles. When your partners or loved ones misbehave themselves, they deserve a good old fashion whack on their bottoms. Fortunately these paddles come in several sizes: small, medium, large (for a good, large ass) and *extra*-large. They are guaranteed to give a nice rosy red look to your loved ones' ass cheeks.

There was a customer who was into such a fetish. She worked at a local high school and taught sex education. Let me share her story with you. Her name was Verna Dobbson and she was in her early sixties. The kids got a real kick out of her. They all thought she was really cool when discussing sex. She even answered her students' questions with a little sauciness.

"Today we're going to talk about safe sex," she began one of her lectures. "Here we have some condoms," she continued, pointing to a display board. "I'm sure you all know what they are for, especially you boys. Who can tell me in detail?"

A young man named Jeffrey raised his hand. Ms. Dobbson acknowledged him and he blurted out, "It's to fill 'em with water and throw 'em out the window on a cop as he's walking by!"

Everyone in class cracked up. "You're so funny," she shot back, quipping, "I clean forgot to laugh! Anyone else want to weigh in? Bill, you have your hand up. What's your answer?"

Bill straightened up and replied quite seriously, "It's so you won't get a girl knocked up."

Ms. Dobbson smiled and said, "Bingo! Good answer. And now, boys and girls, I have a riddle for all of you. What did Eve say to Adam when she didn't want to become pregnant anymore?"

A girl in the back of class raised her hand. "Yes, Ann? Go ahead, stand up so that I can see you better. Your answer is...?"

"You stick me with that thing one more time," Ann mugged, "and I'll kill ya!"

"Correct!" Ms. Dobbson shouted, beaming at the girl. "You get a diaphragm and the Pill for being such a smarty!" She continued asking them riddles and throwing out one-liners. Everyone got a chance to participate. They laughed, learned and had loads of fun in her class.

At night time, however, Verna Dobbson took on another personality. She was known as Spanking Smyrna. Gentlemen from all corners of the city just loved to pay her a call. Why, even little dirty old men came to get a nice ass-whipping.

I heard tell one time than a really elderly man in his late eighties named Henry came into Smyrna's place, walking unsteadily with a cane. He bent his tired body upward to reach her lips and give her a kiss. Smyrna was touched and immediately invited him into her parlor and called for her assistant to serve some tea.

"Would you like some cream and sugar in your tea, my dear Henry?" she asked him coquettishly.

"You bet, my pet, I would love some." After their tea session, he followed her into her bedroom. "Now, Dearie," she snarled, "drop, those pants of yours. How would you like it --- soft, mild or hard?"

Henry grinned and exclaimed, "Gimme the hardest you got, babe, and don't hold back!" He angled his bony body and tossed his cane to one side in order to receive his special punishment.

"Good, you asked for it," she snorted. "I'll paddle that ass of yours so hard that you won't be able to sit down for a week." She whacked away with Henry wincing in pain all the while but never begging her to stop.

And sure enough, what she said came true. The following week whenever he ate dinner with the other occupants at the rest home, he had to sit on a soft pillow. And whenever somebody asked, *What the hell happened to you, Henry old boy*?" he replied, "Spanking Smyrna, that hot babe of mine, left her mark on me!"

21

For those of you who love to have fun and a witty time with sex I recommend you try some of our novelty toys. Take, for instance, the Jack-Off in the Box. You just use the wind up lever on the side of what resembles a small penis and out comes a clown with a big red nose and a huge smile on his face. His trousers connected to long suspenders go up and down. The moment he pops out, he starts talking in the comic voice of Rodney Dangerfield, pulling at his collar and rolling his eyes.

"I can't get no respect, y'know! And boy-oh-boy, do I have a problem. I can't get a hard on, no matter what I do. I even tried waking it up by singing to it, and it goes limp. I tell you, there's no hard prick at all!"

The clown then drops his pants and starts stroking his cock. Next, you push him back into his box and turn the lever again. This time it pops up wearing a skirt and begins singing with a voice similar to the style of Groucho Marx:

"Lydia, Oh Lydia,
My dear sweet Lydia,
How I love to swallow
your vegetable compound.
When I get those
menstrual cramps,
When I'm on the rag ---

Lydia,
Oh Sweet Lydia,
Your compound is for me!"

The toy then raises its skirt and giggles. The Jack-Off In the Box comes complete with a battery charger. I have been told the clown-like figure actually has a story behind it. It comes from an old comic way back in the days of vaudeville and burlesque. Sammy Sunshine was his name and he had everyone rolling in the aisles. He was known for his racy, naughty humor. He had a repertoire of bawdy songs such as

"She was just
about to piddle
when I rammed it
up her spiddle..."

and plenty of risqué jokes like this:

"Question: What did the male astronaut say
to the female astronaut?
Answer: Bend over, honey, and I'll drive
ya to the moon."

At the end of his routine he'd always drop his pants, look down and ask,

"Hey, does Polly want a cracker?"

and a small voice replied, "Any cock'll do!"

His fame spread through the theatrical world. So the next time you whack off, remember fondly about Sammy Sunshine and the amazing Jack-Off in the Box.

22

I did mention a while back about fetishes. There is one in particular that is somewhat fun and people find it rather enjoyable: feet. You heard right --- feet! You may think this a strange way of being aroused, but there are those who just love --- shall we say, get off --- on feet. There is just something alluring in the touch that turns them on.

I'd like to introduce Freddy's Fancy Feet Feathers. They come in a colorful assortment from real ostriches. The mere idea of those lovely feathers flapping across one's feet is quite exciting. They will just titillate those toes of yours! They are very relaxing and give you an erotic, sensual sensation. Ooooh, I'm getting horny just talking about them…whew!

I knew of one fellow who came to the store requesting something for his obsession with feet to fulfill his, you might say, kink. I recommended Freddy's Fancy Feet Feathers. As he looked them over I could see that he was getting excited in more ways than one.

"Ahh," he gasped, "I just adore these feathers and can't wait to give them a nice brushing on some hot feet." He told me his first name was Tim and that some people referred to him as Timmy the Titillating Toes Boy.

"I'm the leader of the local chapter of the F.W.A. --- Feet Worshipers of America," he added. "Our motto is: 'There's nothing like the hot-to-trot taste and feel of a good foot.'" He went on to announce that they have weekly meetings, during which the members take part in an Orgy of Feet Fest.

"Everyone strips off his or her pants or skirt, removes their socks and shoes and we have a wild ass time of it." Tim could hardly catch his breath just talking about these preliminaries. "We have a wide array of feet among our members: small, medium, large, skinny, fat, and so on. The only requirement is that our participants wash their feet so that they don't smell like someone stepped in horse shit. We all like to practice safe sex, you know!" he said, not at all tongue in cheek. "We even use condoms over our toes for those of us who like to toe-fuck our partners. Safe toe sex is even more important!"

Before he left our store he took several packages of Freddy's Fancy Feet Feathers with him. He was beside himself with glee. An F.W.A. member happened to come in the other day and share with me what a wonderful turn-on those feathers were. According to that person everyone in the orgy group has had wild passionate feet sex since Tim bought them.

"We've had to be oh! so careful cleaning all our cum off the feathers afterwards so that we could use them over and over again," the excited individual exclaimed.

It looks like those Fancy Feet Feathers of Freddy's will feather your nest for a long time!

23

There's nothing like being the life of the party. Everyone enjoys a good laugh. With that in mind I'd like to introduce to you Jerry the Farting Fairy. He is a toy pixie who comes complete with a costume, wings and a little cap. You'll have hours of farting fun with him.

Here's how Jerry works: when you press his tummy he farts and says a few funny words for you. His voice is interchangeable and will sound like several comics from the past.

Let me tell you a story about how Jerry the Farting Fairy brought some rollicking fun into a couple of people's lives. Barry and Joan Belvedere were a married couple who lived in the Hollywood Hills. One day they came into the store and wanted something special to include in one of the wild sex parties they were accustomed to throwing frequently. I recommended Jerry the Farting Fairy. They were curious, so I grabbed him, pressed his tummy, and he farted and said mincingly, "Oh, my *good*-ness, you're disss-*gusss*-ting!"

They both cracked up and just loved the little farty one. "Hey," laughed Bob, "that sounds like something Paul Lynde would say!"

Joan was fascinated and said, "Here, let me try!" She squeezed his tummy again. The pixie farted and said meekly, "*Oops! So sorry, I farted! Good night and God ble-e-sss!*"

Joan smiled. "I surely recognize that one," she said brightly. "It's Red Skelton!"

Without hesitating they decided to purchase one of the dolls, took it home and used it for a party they had scheduled for that same evening. They invited some friends over and at one point brought out Jerry the Farting Fairy. He performed all his amazing feats of farting and quipping away in celebrity voices. Everyone laughed themselves silly and had a great time.

Jerry took an unexpected trip the next day. Barry and Joan were beat and decided to sleep in. Jason, their ten year old son, was used to his mom and dad not being awake in the morning. He fixed his own breakfast, washed the dishes, dressed himself and got ready to walk to the bus stop for school. He saw Jerry propped up on a chair near the front door and stuffed him into his backpack. While he was on the bus on the way to school, he became the center of attention with his new found friend.

"Wow, a farting fairy!" one of his buddies shouted while the others snickered. Some of the girls sitting nearby acted appalled and held their noses, for they thought the pixie would smell from all that farting. "He doesn't smell," Jason assured them, "and his farts don't stink either. Just chill!"

In first period his English teacher Miss Jacobs took roll after everyone was seated. Jason held Jerry under his desk to hide him from her view. It was flu season and one or two of his classmates were absent. With that in mind, Jason decided to have a little fun and allow Jerry the Farting Fairy to "answer" for them when their names were called.

"George McDonald?" Miss Jacobs asked. "George McDonald, are you here?" she repeated, scanning the rows of students within her viewing. Jason pressed Jerry firmly and he farted loud and clear.

"*Duh, I farted!*" spouted the voice from Jerry. Everyone in class cracked up and Miss Jacobs looked rather embarrassed. She called a few more names from her roll and all answered in the affirmative until she came to Christopher Vandenberg.

"Christopher Vandenberg?" she asked, again looking out into the sea of young faces. "Are you here? No?" Jason pressed Jerry again even more firmly, and another farting sound rang out. "*Oh, Wilbuuurrrr, forgive me, I'm just an faaaar-ty old ho-o-o-rse!*"

More laughter broke out among the students and their teacher's anger and frustration grew. "All right, who's the one making that noise?!" she demanded to know.

Jason was ready to raise his hand and apologize when he accidentally touched Jerry's tummy again with his other hand, not even squeezing too hard. This time an extremely loud farting sound came out of the doll. "*I eats me spinach 'n am what I yam 'cause that's all that I yam --- I'm Farty the Farting Man --- toot toot*!!" The class turned riotous and it took quite a while for the kids to calm down.

59

After everyone reseated themselves, Miss Jacobs approached Jason's chair, ordered him to stand and gave him an extra assignment. "For being such a smart aleck," she declared, "I want you to go up to the blackboard and write fifty times: '*I will not fart in class*.' That will be your English lesson for today."

So what did Jason and his classmates learn? Don't be such a little smarty farty ass! (Let that be a lesson to us all, right?)

24

Among the other types of kink I must point out is the use of handcuffs. They are very useful for those who enjoy seeing their partner subdued. This can be a sexual turn-on to both the individual who uses the cuffs on his or her partner as well as often for the cuffs' victim.

There was a story about such a man who was known to handcuff his dates. He was notorious especially in leather bars which he frequented. They called him Harry the Happy Handcuff Man. His real name was Johnathan Dresser and he lived in Silverlake, California. I was told about his unusual exploits by someone who had dated him. The evening he had been picked up by Harry the Happy Handcuff Man for the first time over at "The Meat Locker," he went home with him.

"Care for a drink to unwind?" he asked his visitor after they had settled in the living room.

"Yes, I'd love one," his guest replied. After finishing off two highballs, the host excused himself, went into his bathroom and returned moments later wearing a black leather trench coat and hat to match. He then proceeded to go into what could only be described as a police detective routine.

"Ok there, Buddy Boy," he shouted, "you're under arrest. I'm Mike Stone, police detective. Put your hands behind your back --- now!" He then grabbed his guest and dragged him into his bedroom and asked a puzzling question, followed by an even more quizzical command: "Where's your American Express Card? Don't leave home without it!"

He began slowly removing his guest's clothes and went into some weird talk from an old TV show. "Listen, you scum, I'm Sergeant Joe Friday. I have to conduct a strip search on you myself because my partner Bill Gannon is unfortunately not here to assist me."

Taking his hat and coat off, he just stood in his altogether, laughing maniacally. "How did you like it?" he asked when he managed to catch his breath. "Really got ya goin' there for a minute, didn't I?" His grin turned into a serious expression almost immediately. "Now then," he barked, "let me have some of that ass of yours or I'll turn you in for making a pass at a police officer. By the way, it's March 14th, the skies are clear, warm, and it's in the 70s, and we've been working out of Rampart Division."

The individual who told me the story admitted that his host's behavior was a little weird, but he couldn't deny that they both enjoyed themselves tremendously.

And of course justice was done, thanks to that "police detective extraordinaire," Harry the Happy Handcuff Man!

25

Among all the fetishes that exist there is one that really sticks out in my mind. It is known to be rather seductive and erotic when they are worn. They are called shoes. When they are either being worn or seen by someone who has the same shoe attraction, one becomes rather aroused.

May I recommend to you Sofia's Sexy Shoes? They come in several sizes to meet every woman's need. They fit feet to perfection, so they are totally comfortable for wearing on any occasion. The one I'm holding right here reminds me of Dorothy's Ruby Slippers from *The Wizard of Oz*. See how they sparkle? They are designed to be a turn-on for women and men alike.

There was such a woman who was very much into shoes. Listen closely as I tell you her story. Silvana Petrone was her name and she lived in a beach house located along the coast of **Malibu**. She was known to have wild times with her men, especially when they were out on dates. I heard via the grapevine of an incident which took place one summer evening.

Silvana was picked up by Gianni Rosetti, her newly found boyfriend. They drove through the streets of Southern California in his Maserati and ended up in the hills of Griffith Park, not far from the observatory.

"Ah, *cara mia*," Gianni whispered, "how I have

longed for your sweet tender touch." He put Silvana in a very romantic mood. She slipped on her pair of Sofia's Shoes and also began talking in Italian.

"*Amore mio, bacciami presto*!" They kissed and kissed until their lips ached. As a result of thrashing around without holding back in the front seat of Gianni's sports car, nature soon took its course --- *inter*course, that is! They managed to wiggle out of their clothes and shortly were down to their undergarments. Gianni reached over and unhooked her bra while kissing her all over. With the lights of the city blaring beneath them, Gianni maneuvered himself and before you know it, Silvana was shouting with orgasmic abandon, "Yes, yes...yesss!! *Ecco! Si, si, amore mio*," she panted, "stick that *enorme salsiccia* of yours in me deep...deep...deeper...!"

Similar events between them took place several times in the coming weeks in public areas frequented by lovers where all their lustful desires could be fulfilled. In spite of all the pleasure, one unfortunate event involving their passion did take place.

One night she was with Gianni again in his Maserati parked along Pacific Coast Highway. Their lovemaking got steamy as usual and both of them had wiggled out of their clothes until they were naked as jay birds. Silvana slipped on her sparkly red Sophia's Shoes and went into her Italian routine again. She was telling him to pound her harder ("*forte....forte....aah, più forte, amore mio*!) when suddenly she became aware of bright flashing lights behind the car: it was the sheriff! Gianni looked at her with terror on his face.

The officer got out of his car and approached the Maserati, shining his flashlight. When he asked Gianni to roll down his window, he went over the entire interior of the vehicle with his flashlight beam. Hardly noticing that both Silvana and Gianni were stark naked, the sheriff aimed his beam at her shoes and broke out into a huge grin.

"Oh, my goodness," he gasped, "those certainly are hot looking shoes, my dear." He then shone the flashlight on himself, raising his pant leg and revealing that had on the same pair as she did. He screwed up his body and began to sing right there along the highway:

Somewhere over the rainbow
Way up high,
There are shoes that can turn on
Folks just like you and I.

The moral of this story is: Be ever so careful where you shoes may take you!

26

I just love fun and games, don't you? There is one game that you may have heard of: it involves the ol' spinning wheel. A person spins the dial on the wheel and tries to win a prize. Sounds like fun, right?

Well, let me introduce to you a wheel game for adults: Spin Some Sex! In this version the wheel contains pictures and descriptions of various sex acts. The player spins and when the needle lands on a particular place on the wheel, he or she has to perform that act with a partner or partners. And, best of all, there are no winners or losers in this game!

There was a couple whose names were Bob and Alice. They were regular customers of mine. Both were in their early thirties and were looking for a wild sex game for their weekend get-together with another couple. I went over to the shelf and brought out Spin Some Sex. I explained to them how to play it and they just laughed away. I pointed out that it came with a penis which you had to install in the middle of the wheel and which acted as the spinner.

"Oh, we would just love that," exclaimed Bob as they both continued to laugh. "It would be perfect for this weekend. Besides, they said that we might have rain, so this is perfect for a rainy day."

I later heard from the other couple they all had a wild, erotic and very satisfying time at Bob and Alice's party. It had all taken place that previous

Saturday evening at the couple's one-story red brick home located on the outskirts of Berkeley. The invited guests had gathered around the fireplace when Bob brought out the game.

"Hey, guys, move in closer. Alice and I just bought a new game that's just perfect for the four of us." He opened the box and there was a colorful wheel with a large cock and balls which they had to attach to the middle to be used as the spinner. Whatever it landed on the wheel, you and whomever you were with or chose as your partner had to perform the sex act depicted. All of them giggled and just loved the idea.

The other couple they had invited was Ted and Janice. "OK, you guys," Bob said, "let's flip a coin to see who goes first." Bob won the flip, smiled from ear to ear at the idea of what they were participating in and proceeded to spin the old cock wheel. It landed on ORAL! Everyone busted out laughing when Bob glanced lustfully at Ted.

"Hey, Ted!" he blurted out. "Care for some head?"

Ted grinned and replied, "I'd love some, Bob. To tell you the truth, I haven't had a nice blow job in weeks."

His wife Janice look pissed and not a little confused by her husband's remarks. She went into a bit of a tizzy. "What the hell are you saying?!" she snapped. "Isn't the head I give you good enough?"

"Well, yeah," Ted responded sheepishly, "but somehow it's good to have a man around to do it and, you know…, spice things up a little!"

Bob's wife saw them having such a great time, felt sorry for Janice and decided to break it up by joining in. "Say there," she said in an authoritative tone, "back off and gimme that nice juicy cock of yours. I'll show you all what a genuine blow job is like."

Before you know it, Alice pushed Bob aside was going hot and heavily at Ted. Next, Janice raised her hand and shouted, "Don't leave me out! I'd like a go, too! Let me spin again to see where it lands."

"Okie dokie!" Bob shouted. "Spin that damn cock already!" Janice gave it a good hefty spin and it landed on FUCKING. She hurriedly slipped off her dress, grabbed a hold of Bob's cock and began rubbing it furiously. "Ready for a nice lay, honey?" he asked between gasps of pleasure. The two of them were going at it with such enthusiasm that it forced Ted and Alice to look over at them in wonder.

Ted asked her, "I wonder if it'd be OK for us to join in the fun?" He reached over to spin the ol' wiener again and this time it landed on ORGY. They all bunched up and had a fucking good time for the remainder of the evening.

Always remember this burning question: Who knows where the cock and balls will land and strike next?!?

27

There are a lot of strange, bizarre kinks and fetishes out there. People just love to indulge in wild and crazy kinds of sex. The one that sticks out in my mind is voyeurism: the act of spying on someone while they are having sex.

For that reason we do have one product that really fits the bill: Pete's "Peeping Tom" Periscope. It is in the shape of a dildo and keeps you in the mood while watching whomever you want to see fucking.

Just the other day a gentleman came into our store. He took me aside and shared with me a special turn-on he had. He introduced himself as Fred and he was a local pastor from a prominent church in town. He confided to me that he secretly enjoyed watching people having sex, especially in public. "I just love going to parks at night and searching for couples getting it on in their cars. I hide behind trees or crouch down behind bushes and watch them thrashing away. It gives me a real hard-on."

I noticed him salivating as he talked to me. I directed him over to our section where the periscopes are displayed. I explained to him that one of them would be perfect for any sightseer who appreciates the sexual arts as he does. He loved the idea and bought one.

One evening Ted decided to go out when the sun was just about to set. He chose the palisades above the beach in Santa Monica which was known to be rather notorious for such activity. He alighted from his car and walked over to a huge tree with a thick trunk. Lo and behold, there was a car parked just beyond the tree. Staying hidden, Pastor Fred quickly pulled out his Pete's "Peeping Tom" Periscope and adjusted the focus button to obtain a sharper image.

"Ah-ha-ha," he murmured giddily. "This is great! Now I can see what's going on even closer and stay totally concealed from view." He began drooling as he watched the couple remove every stitch of clothing they had been wearing. "Wow," he thought, not able to take his eyes off them, "they're both buck naked. It looks rather interesting what's going on."

Raw lust began to get the best of Pastor Fred. He quickly whipped out his old weenie and began jerking off with his right hand while manipulating the periscope with his left. "Mmm!" he hummed. "Nice tits on that dame, and boy oh boy, what a huge cock and set of balls that guy has!" After a while Pastor Fred packed up the periscope and sauntered away from the area, walking as nonchalantly as he could in order not to attract any attention.

Remembering the spot along the palisades, the horny man continued going out night after night at the same time for quite a long while. He always managed to slink away undetected, but the tide was about to turn against him.

One night when there was no moon above, he walked in near darkness, heading toward the wooded area and the tree which had become so

70

familiar. Turning down the wrong path he reached a dead end and was barely able to make out a sign: NUDIST AREA - PARTICIPANTS ONLY - NO TRESPASSERS OR LOOKILOOS ALLOWED.

Well, Pastor Fred couldn't pass up an opportunity like this! He had to find a way, however, to ditch his periscope before walking up to the entry point and asking if he could join in. Someone tapped him on the shoulder and a voice rang out in the dark, asking "What business do you have here? Do you want to join us?"

Pastor Fred stepped back, and a flashlight beam suddenly shone in his face. He nodded slightly, even though he was a little startled at the thought of what might happen if his parishioners found out where he was and how he was gratifying his pastime proclivities.

"Well, come in already," a naked man said, smiling. "You'll have to take off all your clothes right away, though. And whatever you do, don't let anybody see that periscope you've got there. Wrap it up in your clothing and I'll store it in a locker in the main office. It's down the way. I'll bring back a towel for you, too."

Ted did as instructed, hurriedly shedding his clothes and making certain that the periscope was wrapped up and undetected in the bundled garments. When he was handed a towel, he instinctively wrapped it around his private parts, still shy about exhibiting himself fully naked. As his eyes

71

adjusted to the dark he became aware of several people frolicking in the area. He could see the gleaming teeth of plenty of nice smiles.

"Hey, what's that thing sticking out from your towel, man?" a young man asked in passing. Taken by surprise Ted answered meekly, "It's my dick."

"Whew!" another man gasped as curious onlookers assembled. "That's a whopper you've got there, baby. You must be pretty gifted. You're new here, huh? Who the hell are you, anyway?"

Fred gulped and replied, "I'm Pastor Fred from the Holy Mother of Consumption Church."

The crowd stifled their laughter. "Oh-ho!" a female voice tittered. "*Another* holy man graces our little group. It's a nice night for running around naked, isn't it, Pastor? I don't suppose you've run into Father Martin yet, have you?"

Fred agreed that the night was nice, but he was perplexed by the presence of another church person. No sooner was he ready to slip away than a large man pushed his way through the crowd of young people. "It's great for cock watching, too," his voice boomed. The priest himself, the one they called Father Martin, reached into his own towel and pulled out a Pete's "Peeping Tom" Periscope.

Pastor Fred was shocked and cried, "I didn't know you were into the same thing!"

"Oh, heavens yes! I just love to see naked beauty. Come, Fred, let me show you around and point out my special secret spying place."

Fred thought that sounded like hot fun. He turned to the priest and asked, "Would you mind telling me what kind of sex you like to watch?"

"Oh," Father Martin crowed, "any cock'll do!" They both looked at each other and laughed themselves silly.

That just goes to prove that Pete's "Peeping Tom" Periscope can turn out to be quite a heavenly gift, no matter what denomination you belong to!

28

Since I am on the subject of kink and fetishes, there is one that is rather strange, but oh! so much fun. It gives one a special thrill: exhibitionism. People who are into this get turned on by showing off, shall we say, their pride and joy --- that is, their most private parts in public. I knew such a person. Let me share his wild adventure with you.

One day, a man in his early forties came to see me. He told me about his turn-on and how he just loved to show himself off in public for everyone to see. It seemed that he wanted something different and eye-catching. I walked him over to our special section and showed him some attire which would fit him to a "T." It was called Eddie's Exhibitionist Ensemble. It consisted of a long coat and a see-through jockstrap.

"Wow," he roared, "this is fucking fantastic." I explained to him that the coat flaps can easily be adjusted so that he could expose himself to whomever he wished while still protecting his private parts. He bought the outfit without hesitating and was very happy indeed.

Well, the next morning he had plans for his new found attire. He was going to visit his favorite place: the hills and woods located outside the city of Auburn. "Let's see," he reflected, "I'll just put on my jockstrap and cover it with this long coat." He drove to his destination and parked.

Stepping out of the vehicle, he could barely contain himself. "Let's see where I can show myself off," he thought excitedly. "Ah, I know. I'll pick one of the trails and find a bush to hide behind." He discovered the perfect spot and waited for his unsuspecting victims. In a short while he heard someone walked up the trail. This was the exhibitionist's moment of excitement. Jumping out in the middle of the trail, he encountered a young man. He smiled and said, "Hi there! Nice day, isn't it?" He quickly opened the flaps of his coat, exposing the transparent jockstrap. "Have a good one!" he added cheerily and scampered away.

Several more hikers came down the trail and our exhibitionist friend repeated the same routine. Each of his victims expressed shock, anger and disgust. There was, however, one glaring exception.

It was nearly noon and a trim young lady in an attractive blue blouse with slacks to match wandered down the path toward the bush. Our exhibitionist enthusiast jumped out as usual and shouted, "Surprise, surprise!"

The young lady rolled her eyes and remarked, "Oh, that's a cute wee-wee you've got there. And guess what? I've got a surprise for you." She fished out a small portfolio from her pocket, flipped it open and showed him her police badge. "You're under arrest for lewd conduct. We've been getting reports at headquarters all morning about you and that wee-wee of yours."

As he turned and placed his hands behind his back for her to cuff him, he said in protest, "I resent you calling my private part a wee-wee. I always refer to it as my cock."

Taken a second look at him, she giggled uncontrollably. "I've seen many a cock in this line of work," she declared, barely able to keep a straight face, "and I can tell you beyond a shadow of a doubt that yours is definitely a *wee-wee*!"

Poor guy! It looks like his exhibitionism days have been cut short. Remember, always be careful to whom you show yourself off!

29

I just love having fun and a good time, don't you? Well, there is one game that I have over here and it's just one for you. It will make you laugh and enjoy life. The game is Pin the Cock on the Asshole. Just the thought of it cracks me up.

Here we have a 3-D picture of an ass with an actual deep hole in the middle. Your mission, should you choose to accept it, is to take your own cock and balls and try sticking it right inside the asshole. If you're female you can either use a dildo or grab your boyfriend's cock and try to place it inside the ass. You'll have loads of fun sticking the ol' pecker in between those ass cheeks.

There were these two hillbilly guys who came to town every so often. Jeb and Jethro were farmhands and they lived on a ranch nearby. One day they both visited my store and were talking among themselves.

"Hey, Jeb?"

"Yeah, Jethro? Whad y'all want?"

"I've been a-lookin' around this here store for a li'l ol' game to play over at the farmhouse. This one here is lookin' mighty fine."

"Lemme take a gander. I'll be right on over thar."

Jeb met Jethro over at the display and they both laughed so hard, they sounded like two mules. "Let's try it out. I wanna see if we can aim our big ol' cocks inside thar."

They bought the game and as they were leaving I

overheard one of them say, "Gee, Jethro, I can't wait t' see what happens."

"Me neither, Jeb. Maybe I'll have Betty Lou take her hand and guide my dick right into that thar hole. Won't that be a humdinger..."

When they arrived back at the ranch they rushed to their room, closed the door and tried it out. "Lemme see here..., I'll jus' place this here pichur of the asshole on the dresser and try puttin' my good ol' cock inside of it."

Jethro went up to the ass and tried sticking it in. "Hot damn, that thar feels mighty nice, just like one o' them real ones."

"Shit, Jethro, you ain't one o' them thar queers, are ya? I'd a-thought you'd be fixin' t' put it up Betty Lou's behind!"

Jethro smirked. "Okay, smart ass, why don't you try it? Bethcha yore gonna like it."

Jeb scratched his head and replied, "Don't mind if'n I do, but I am goin' a li'l blind here and need them glasses the doctor gimme las' year."

Jethro planned on playing a mean trick on Jeb. "What say, Jeb, we take this here game outdoors in the sunshine so's you can see a li'l better? I'll go and get your glasses fer ya."

Jeb nodded and exclaimed, "Awright, but hurry up thar. I'm jus' itch'n to try stickin' it in." Little did poor dumb Jeb know that sneaky Jethro had no plans to ever go and fetch his glasses. Jeb groped around outside for a while. "Hey, you varmint! I'm out here already. Where th' hell 're y'all at anyway?"

Jethro yelled to him from the other side of the yard. "Over here by the cows and mules." Poor Jeb still couldn't see a thing. "Where ya at and where's my glasses?" he shouted angrily.

"Oh," Jethro replied sheepishly, "I couldn't find 'em. You must've mislaid 'em. But don't fret, I'll just watch fer ya. Trust me, jus' mosey on over and have yer cock 'n balls all ready to stick 'em right in between them ass cheeks."

Jeb put his hands out and started feeling around, squinting the whole time. "I can't see a friggin' thang, Jethro."

Jethro snickered to himself and replied, "Don't go frettin' none, Jeb. I put a li'l hair around it so's you can aim better, Go on ahead, try it out. Yore right on top of 'er, boy."

Jeb touched the little tufts of hair and grinned. "Hey, thanks, son," he said. "I can feel that thar hair you put 'round it right in front o' me." He took his cock and tried aiming it, but felt something moving in the process. "Lordee," he cried, "somethin's powerful wrong here. I'll try puttin' it agin..."

He thrust it forcefully this time and soon found himself flying through the air clear over to the far side of the yard smackdab in the pig pen. He didn't know what hit him. Everything appeared hazier than ever, though he could clearly hear Jethro laughing until his sides split.

"What in tarnation's wrong with you, Jethro?"

asked Jeb, puzzled and not a little angry. "Whad're ya laughin' fer?"

Jethro calmed down and answered, "Margaret the Mule shore didn't cottin' t' havin' yer dick 'n balls stuck up her behind. She gave y'all the biggest kick I ever sawed in all my days. But when y'all landed in that pigpen, I plumb near died laughin'. Yer all covered with mud, boy, and ya smell real bad."

Jeb lifted himself up, brushed himself off and yelled, "Now yer gonna get whupped, son, and I don' give a lick if'n I can't see where I'm a-goin'. I'm gonna git ya but good!" And he ended up chasing Jethro around the barnyard until both of them managed to fall into the pigpen.

Poor ol' Jeb! What a nasty trick Jethro played on him. But in the end he got his comeuppance. It just goes to show you that you should always be careful what you're sticking your cock into --- you may get a real kick out of it!

+ + + + + +

As I am looking over at the counter here I see more customers coming in. They can't seem to get enough of our items for their sexual enjoyment. I hate to leave you, but I must get back to business. It's been such an honor to have served up some juicy stories for you and lots of fun revealing so many delightful secrets. Thank you for your attention, and I hope to see you again real soon.

Remember, whenever you think of sex and need that extra sensual touch, please drop by the store. You'll find me (or someone like me) if you search far and wide enough. Until then ---

Auf Wiedersehen,
Au Revoir
and tell 'em that
Fifi sent you!

Made in the USA
Columbia, SC
13 February 2024

31350223R00049